The Magic School Bus Rides Again

Monster Power

by
Judy Katschke

BRANCHES

SCHOLASTIC INC.

Ms. Frizzle's Class

Jyoti

Arnold

Ralphie

Wanda

Keesha

Dorothy Ann

Carlos

Tim

TABLE OF CONTENTS

© 2018 Scholastic Inc.
Based on the television series *The Magic School Bus: Rides Again*.
© 2017 MSB Productions, Inc.
Based on *The Magic School Bus*® series © Joanna Cole and Bruce Degen.
All rights reserved.

Published by Scholastic Inc., *Publishers since 1920*.
SCHOLASTIC, THE MAGIC SCHOOL BUS, BRANCHES, and logos are trademarks and/or registered trademarks of Scholastic Inc.

Library of Congress Cataloging-in-Publication Data available

ISBN 978-1-338-23213-4 (hardcover) / ISBN 978-1-338-19444-9 (paperback)

10 9 8 7 6 5 4 3 2 1   18 19 20 21 22
Printed in China   38

First edition, January 2018
Edited by Marisa Polansky
Book design by Jessica Meltzer

CHAPTER 1

ARNOLD'S SCARY TALE

The day had just begun for Ms. Frizzle's class. But Arnold already had a story. He was telling the class about a monster from a scary movie he had seen.

"It was unbelievable!" Arnold told his friends. "It had fourteen eyeballs and giant, nasty **tentacles**!"

1

"Aww, I've never heard of anything like that. He sounds like the last of his kind," Wanda said. "He must be lonely."

Arnold knew that Wanda's passion was saving all living beings. He didn't know that included monsters!

"Don't feel bad for him, Wanda," Arnold said. "He belches sulfuric acid and shoots flames from his nose!"

Tim wrinkled his brow. "Sul-fu-what?" he asked.

Dorothy Ann had an answer for everything, and if she didn't know it, she looked it up! "Sulfuric acid," she explained. "It's an acid that's super strong."

"In that case," Tim said, "those belches have got to hurt!"

Ralphie walked over to join his friends.

"Belches? Guys, if you have something to say about me," Ralphie said. "say it to my face."

"We're talking about someone else with deadly burps, Ralphie," Tim explained. "It's a monster Arnold saw in a movie."

"But burps are my thing!" joked Ralphie.

Arnold continued to describe the monster. "It only comes out at night," he said. "It loves **pollution**, which helps it grow bigger and bigger until the sky is blotted out by its blotty blottiness!"

"Loves pollution?" Wanda asked. "Who would love stinky air and dirty water?"

"The Blot Monster, that's who," Arnold answered. "And the only thing that can stop it is light."

Arnold waited for gasps, shivers, or maybe screams, but all he got were smiles and a few chuckles.

"That sounds like a fun movie, Arnold," Ralphie admitted, "but I don't think it's real."

It felt real to Arnold.

"From now on I'm staying inside with the lights on," said Arnold. "There is no way I'll sleep in the dark ever again."

Arnold glanced around the classroom. "Speaking of sleep, why does everyone have sleeping bags and backpacks?"

Suddenly, a rope dropped from the ceiling down to the floor. The kids watched as their teacher Ms. Frizzle shimmied down the rope!

She landed with a hop in the middle of the classroom. Liz, the class lizard, climbed down behind her.

"Good morning, campers!" Ms. Frizzle said. She was wearing a shirt with a tree and mountains, and she had a star-shaped

compass around her neck. "Are you ready?"

Tim, Wanda, Dorothy Ann, and Ralphie nodded their heads. They were ready. So were Keesha, Carlos, and Jyoti.

Their magical class trips were always an awesome surprise. Ms. Frizzle had taken them everywhere from an undersea adventure to inside a volcano. And *that's* exactly what worried Arnold.

"Um . . . ready for what, Ms. Frizzle?" Arnold asked.

"Adventure! Campfire!" Ms. Frizzle replied. "To sleep all night in the really dark wilderness!"

Arnold froze. "Dark?" he asked.

"Maybe we'll see a giant spider!" Carlos said, smiling. "Or a huge snake!"

"Or worse," Arnold mumbled. *How could his friends sleep in the dark wilderness? They would become a snack for the Blot Monster!* thought Arnold.

Arnold knew he had to do something fast. He waved his hand in the air and shouted, "Ms. Frizzle! Ms. Frizzle!"

"Yes, Arnold?" Ms. Frizzle asked.

"I can't go!" Arnold cried. "I cannot go on this class trip!"

CHAPTER 2
FRIGHT LIGHT

Why can't you go on our trip, Arnold?" Ms. Frizzle asked.

"Because I don't have my sleeping bag or my fireproof pj's," he said.

"Oh," Ms. Frizzle said. "You mean *these* fireproof pj's?" Ms. Frizzle held up blue-and-white striped pajamas. Behind her was a pile of Arnold's camping gear. "Your mom dropped off everything when she saw you left them behind, Arnold."

"I must have forgotten them on purpose," Arnold said. "Because I didn't want to face the Blot Monster."

"Sounds like a fun campfire story," said Ms. Frizzle. "I can't wait to hear it!"

Ms. Frizzle turned to the others. "Okay, class," she boomed. "Let's get camping!"

Arnold watched as his classmates grabbed their gear and headed for the bus.

Arnold couldn't go just yet. He had a job to do! He went around the room and collected as many lights as he could possibly hold!

Where there is light, there is no Blot Monster, Arnold told himself. *And I'm not taking any chances!*

Arnold dragged his giant bag of lights to the parking lot. Ms. Frizzle's Magic School Bus was ready to roll. Or swim. Or fly. Or do whatever surprise Ms. Frizzle had in store.

Ms. Frizzle's bus was like no other school bus in the world. It could **transform** itself into whatever Ms. Frizzle needed.

Ms. Frizzle, the kids, and Liz hoped aboard and buckled their seat belts.

"Okay, bus," Ms. Frizzle called out, "do your stuff! And, class, get ready for an **enlightening** experience!"

The Magic School Bus swirled and whirled until it disappeared!

POOF!

The bus reappeared above a long, rolling river. A giant parachute popped out the top of the bus, making it drift slowly downward.

"And down we go," Ms. Frizzle called, "to the most perfect campground."

That sounds nice, thought Arnold.

"Next to the most perfect giant waterfall!" she added.

Not so nice!

The bus was about to splash down when—POOF—its wheels **inflated** into air-filled rafts!

The bus landed gently on the water. But Ralphie heard something that sounded like WOOOOOSH. He gulped.

"Uh, what's that sound?" he asked.

"Why, that's just the beautiful sounds of the waterfall, Ralphie!"

That did not make Ralphie feel much better.

Tim pointed out the window and shouted, "There it is! And we're picking up speed!"

The bus moved closer and closer to the roaring waterfall.

"AAAAAAAAAAAAAAHHHHHHH!" the class shouted.

The Magic School Bus headed straight for the giant waterfall.

But just as the bus tipped toward the falls, Ms. Frizzle pulled a handle. It sprouted airplane wings!

The bus flew far away from the falls, and the kids cheered. "Whooooa! Awesome!"

Ms. Frizzle stuck her head out the window and said one of her usual jokes. "Like my great-aunt Nettie used to say, 'I love camping. It's in-tents!'"

The Magic School Bus landed on a grassy, open campground. Now that the kids were safe, they were ready to have some fun. Jyoti reached for her bike, and Keesha and Tim grabbed balls and kites.

Arnold wasn't worried about fun. He only had room to worry about one thing—the Blot Monster!

"Why did you bring all those lights, Arnold?" Jyoti asked.

"It's the only thing that will scare off the Blot Monster," Arnold explained.

"Well, I hate to break it to you," Jyoti said, "but your plan has a problem."

Problem? Arnold hated problems almost as much as pepper, pollen, and pressure!

"We're in the middle of nowhere," Jyoti explained. "How are you going to plug in the lights?"

Arnold stared at Jyoti. "Oh no!" he cried. "How did I miss that? But if we don't have lights, how will we keep away the evil Blot Monster?"

CHAPTER 3

ROTORS AND BOATERS

Arnold had a big problem but he had an idea of who might help: Ms. Frizzle!

"There has to be a way to power up these lights," Arnold said. "At home, I'd just plug them into the wall."

"At home, a **power plant** delivers **electricity** through power lines to your house," Ms. Frizzle said, "but there are no power lines in the woods."

Arnold sighed. He was afraid Ms. Frizzle would say that!

"But then some people make their own power instead of getting it from a power plant," Ms. Frizzle said, "like Dorothy Ann's family."

Dorothy Ann, or D.A. as they called her, was using her tablet to identify wildlife around the campground.

"Hey, D.A.!" Arnold said. "Where does your family plug in their lights?"

"In the wall?" Dorothy Ann asked, confused.

"No," Arnold said, "I mean, how do you guys get your power?"

"Mostly from the sun. That's called solar energy," Dorothy Ann said. "But we also have a generator for backup."

"A what-erator?" Arnold asked.

"A *this*-erator!" Ms. Frizzle said.

She turned toward the bus and—WHAM! A giant screen appeared from the side of bus. A **projector** made a whirring noise.

"Pass the popcorn, kids," Ms. Frizzle said. "It's showtime!"

A black-and-white movie flickered on. Arnold was glad it was not about the Blot Monster, or any monster. Instead it was about—

"The generator!" an announcer boomed.

The movie showed the inside of a gasoline generator. Arnold and Dorothy Ann had never seen anything like it before.

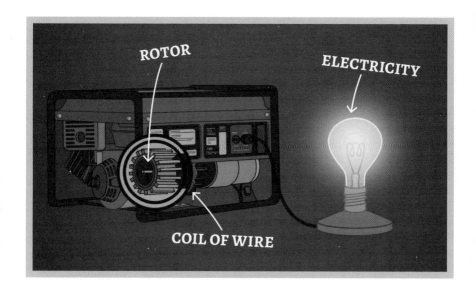

ROTOR

ELECTRICITY

COIL OF WIRE

"A spinning rotor and a coil of wire are inside the generator," the announcer explained. "They work together. That is how ultimate power is created! Energy becomes electricity."

"Power! That's what I need!" Arnold shouted. "Where can I get a generator exactly like that?"

"We might have an old generator here," Ms. Frizzle said, "from before the bus went solar."

She popped open the trunk and rummaged through some old junk. She pulled out a machine shaped like a big box. "Here we go!"

"Perfect!" Arnold said. "If I set this up now, we just might survive the night."

"Well, let's hope so, Arnold," said Ms. Frizzle.

"Fill 'er up, Liz!" Arnold said. "We're going to need a lot of gasoline to run this thing all night."

Arnold had set up the generator and put lights all around the campground. He watched as Liz poured gasoline into the machine.

"This has got to work. Right, Liz?" Arnold asked.

"Arnold!" Jyoti called as she ran over. "I made a picnic down by the water. Come on!"

"But I have stuff to do," Arnold said.

"No, what you have to do is have fun!" Jyoti said.

"Fun? But the night is coming, and I haven't even tested the lights," Arnold groaned. Jyoti dragged him away from the generator and down to the water where the other kids were having a pizza picnic.

Just then, they heard Ms. Frizzle's voice. "Do you want to see something powerful, class?" She was aboard the bus, which had transformed into a big boat.

"All aboard, class!" Ms. Frizzle shouted.

"Guys, I don't have time for this. The lights aren't set up, the sun's going down, and the monster—"

"Oh, Arnold," said Ralphie, "live a little."

Arnold groaned as the class boarded the bus. The kids stood on the front of the boat. It was moving fast.

"Wow, the boat keeps moving even though the engine is off," said Tim.

"Hmmm. It's getting pushed by the flow of water from the waterfall," said Dorothy Ann.

"Talk about powerful!" said Jyoti.

"Well, let's feel what we see! Hit it, Liz!" Ms. Frizzle shouted.

Captain Liz turned on the engine and steered right for the waterfall. Water from the falls rained down on the kids' heads.

"Whoa," said Carlos. "That is a *lot* of water!"

"And a lot of power," said Ms. Frizzle.

"Yeah, uh, very nice," said Arnold. But he wasn't interested in the water. He had a lot on his mind! "Can we please get back now? So I can save us all?"

"Sure, Arnold," said Ms. Frizzle. "Our work here is done."

CHAPTER 4
POWER TRIP

Back at the campgrounds, Arnold powered up the generator, and it sputtered to life. Then, he flipped the switch and the lights turned on.

"Phew! Now I can get some sleep, Liz. Thanks to the Official Arnold Perlstein Monster Scaring **Perimeter**!" said Arnold.

"Good news, everybody!" Arnold shouted to his classmates. "I've saved us from the Blot Monster! The generator burns gasoline to make the rotor spin through a wire coil that makes electricity, which powers these lights, which will save our lives!"

Arnold waited for applause, but it was silent.

"You're welcome," Arnold said with a sigh.

"You know, Arnold," Jyoti said, "that is pretty awesome."

"Thank you, Jyoti!" Arnold cried. "I'm glad somebody appreciates all my work."

"Wait!" said Keesha. "Something doesn't smell right. This generator stinks!"

"What do you mean? The generator is working great," said Arnold.

"No! I mean something actually stinks." Keesha waved smoke away from the generator. "The generator's spewing **exhaust** from the engine," she said. "Gasoline creates pollution."

"And the exhaust is polluting our campground," Carlos added. "Yuck!"

"Nobody likes pollution," Keesha said.

Arnold was about to agree when he had a scary thought.

"You know, Keesha, I wouldn't be too sure," he said. "There's one thing that actually does love pollution: the Blot Monster!"

CHAPTER 5

QUICK LIKE THE WIND

Arnold and Liz stared at the generator. Arnold was back to square one. He needed to find clean energy or the Official Arnold Perlstein Monster Scaring Perimeter would be doomed.

"Come on, Arnold," Carlos said. "You're totally stressing over this. Take a break."

"I can't," Arnold insisted. "I have to find a new clean energy source to power my lights or we'll be monster chow!"

"Go fly a kite," Carlos said.

"Ouch," Arnold said. "That was harsh."

"No, I mean let's fly an actual kite," Carlos said. "I brought a bunch. It'll be fun."

"But I have to make the generator run without causing pollution," Arnold said. "I have to think of the needs of everyone here."

"And we need you to have some fun," Carlos said.

Just then, Ms. Frizzle called to the class.

"Class, I've got a breezy idea!"

"Instead of flying kites, why not become the kites?" she said.

"Let's do it!" Carlos cheered.

"Let's not," Arnold mumbled.

PFFT! PFFT! PFFT! The Magic School Bus spit out the kids one by one. They were wearing full-body kite suits. Each suit was attached to the back of the bus with a super-long cord.

"I knew I should have stayed home today," Arnold groaned as the wind lifted him high into the sky.

"Whoa!" Dorothy Ann laughed as a gust of wind spun her around. "I can feel the wind holding us up!"

"Who knew wind was so strong? It has so much power!" Wanda said.

"How fast do you think the wind is blowing up here?" Ralphie asked. "Because I want to brag about it later."

Dorothy Ann loved pulling up facts in a flash. This time she pulled out a special device for measuring wind.

"According to my anemometer," Dorothy Ann said, "the wind here is blowing at twenty-two miles per hour."

"D.A., you carry a wind measuring thing in your pocket at *all* times?" Ralphie asked.

"Obviously," Dorothy Ann said. "What do you carry?"

"Emergency pizza!" Ralphie said, taking a bite of a cheesy slice.

Arnold wasn't thinking about pizza as he drifted past his friends. All he could think about was the Official Arnold Perlstein Monster Scaring Perimeter back on the ground.

"Why am I up here?" asked Arnold. "I've still got to find a way to spin that rotor!"

As he hung in midair, Arnold glanced down. Everything seemed so small from way up high. Then he spotted one tiny object that gave him a big idea—Keesha's bike!

"Ms. Frizzle, I need to get down!" Arnold shouted, waving his arms and legs. "I have an idea that will save us all!"

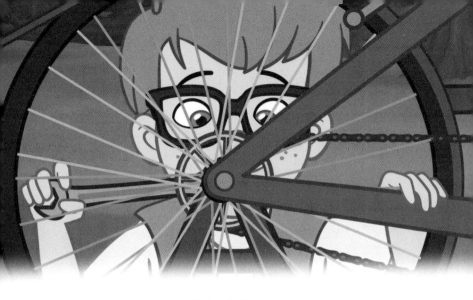

CHAPTER 6

FULL TEAM AHEAD

Back on the ground, Arnold was hard at work. "That should do it," Arnold said as he turned a wrench. Keesha's bike wheel was attached to the rotor of the generator. "I'm going to use the power of Keesha's bike to make the rotor spin, which will power the generator and turn on these lights. Or . . . uh . . . that's the idea. Liz, it's time for a test run!"

Arnold sat on the bike and gripped the handlebars. Liz blew a whistle from the top of the bike handles. Arnold began to pedal the bike and spin the wheel, then the generator's rotor began spinning, too!

"See? We don't need gasoline to spin the rotor," Arnold told Liz. "I can make it spin with nonpolluting kid energy."

The lights flickered on and Arnold cheered, "Yes! We did it! Take that, Blot Monster!"

Liz blew a whistle to keep time. Arnold pumped the pedals faster and faster.

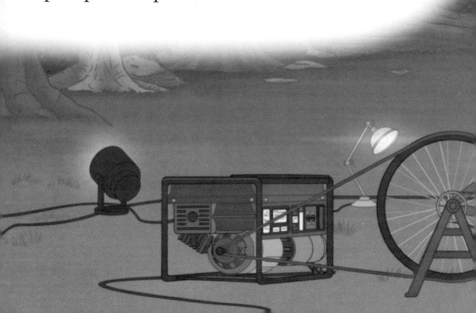

"I hope I'll be able to keep this going," Arnold said between huffs and puffs.

Arnold pedaled and pedaled, but he was losing steam. Just then, his classmates appeared.

"Look at the lights!" Jyoti cheered. "Arnold did it!"

"Yeah, but look at Arnold," Wanda said as she pointed to Arnold. He was out of breath.

"He must really believe in this Blot Monster," Carlos said with a sigh.

"I don't," Keesha said. "Come on, you guys. A monster?"

"I've seen a lot of monster movies," Tim admitted, "and the kid who says there's no monster gets eaten first."

Tim drew a sketch of the Blot Monster and held it up. The kids gathered around to see the hairy, scary beast.

"Is that what the Blot Monster looks like?" Wanda said with a gasp. "It's so . . ."

"So cool!" Carlos yelled.

"He's got tentacles?" Jyoti asked. "And he lives on land?"

Keesha looked at the monster sketch. She had to admit it was crazy-creepy!

"Maybe we should help Arnold," Keesha said. "Just in case."

Arnold did need help. The lights on his generator were fading. And so was he!

"Take a break, Arnold," Ralphie urged him. "I've got it from here."

The kids in Ms. Frizzle's class took turns pedaling Keesha's bike. They kept the generator running. But they couldn't keep themselves from running out of juice!

"Another . . . few . . . minutes," Tim said with a gasp from the ground. "And I'll be ready . . . to . . . go again."

"We can't keep this up all night," said Keesha.

"Guys, we have no choice," Arnold said. "We must keep pedaling!"

Arnold dragged himself back on the bike. The bike began to make weird, squeaky noises. He pedaled with all his might until— BOOOOOING—a wheel popped off!

BOO_OO_OING!

Everyone watched wide-eyed as the bicycle wheel rolled away.

"My bike!" Keesha cried. "Quick! Grab the wheel!"

Keesha led the chase after the runaway wheel. Arnold watched as it bounced toward the river.

"Our only clean power source is gone!" Arnold wailed. "Without lights, how will we stop the Blot Monster? We're doomed!"

CHAPTER 7
THE WHEEL DEAL

Everyone chased after Keesha's wheel as fast as they could. The kids ran as it headed down a hill and nearly out of sight. Ralphie jumped for it, but it rolled out of reach. The wheel hit a tree and bounced back straight at Keesha and Tim. "Woooa!" they screamed and ducked. Then it rolled toward Wanda and toward the baby squirrel by her foot.

Arnold pointed and screamed, "Wanda, quick! Grab the—"

Wanda scooped up the baby squirrel. Phew!

"I was going to say 'wheel,'" said Arnold.

But the wheel didn't stop. It headed toward the water and so did the kids. Then—SPLASH— it rolled straight into the waterfall and got stuck between two rocks. Even though it was stuck, it kept spinning.

"Whoa!" Wanda exclaimed. "Look at it go!"

"Cool!" Jyoti said. "The power of the rushing water is really making the wheel spin."

"It's not doing us any good in there," Arnold said. He dropped down on his belly near the water. "Somebody hold on to my feet! I'll try to grab it!"

Arnold waded into the water and grabbed the wheel.

"We have to get back to camp," Arnold said. "It's getting darker."

Arnold lifted the wheel over his head and led the race back to camp. He ran super fast as if his life depended on it! Then—WHOOSH—a gust of wind slowed him way down.

"Wind . . . super . . . strong," Arnold said with a gasp.

The powerful wind held Arnold back like a brick wall. He gripped the wheel so hard his fingers hurt. Suddenly, an even stronger gust yanked the wheel from his hands!

"Noooooo!" Arnold cried.

The wind lifted the bicycle wheel into the air.

"Look at the wheel! It's still spinning!" Jyoti said.

The wheel kept spinning in midair. When the wind died down, the wheel dropped to the ground. Ralphie grabbed it and began to run.

"Go, Ralphie, go!" Arnold shouted. "Lives are at stake!"

Finally, they made it back to camp.

Jyoti grabbed the wheel. She was great at putting things together and making them work.

"I've got this part," said Jyoti. She attached the wheel to the bicycle and screwed it on tight. She gave it a spin. The generator lights flickered on.

"Okay, it still works," Jyoti said. "Tim, hop on and start pedaling."

But Tim wasn't going anywhere. "Can't," he said. "I'm too tired."

"Someone has to get on the bike," Dorothy Ann said. "Any volunteers?"

Arnold didn't raise his hand. Neither did Keesha, Ralphie, Wanda, Carlos, Jyoti, or Tim.

"Sorry, D.A.," Wanda said. "We've been playing and pedaling and running all day. We're all beat."

Arnold was beat, too. But he knew they had to beat a certain monster before dark!

"We have to do something," Arnold said. "Otherwise we're going to get a visit from the Blot Monster."

Ms. Frizzle walked over, holding a spinning pinwheel. "Hang in there, class," she said. "You'll figure it out."

"How, Ms. Frizzle?" Arnold asked.

"Use your brain power!" Ms. Frizzle replied.

Brain . . . power?

Arnold put his brain to work. That's when something suddenly clicked.

"Brain *power*!" Arnold cried. "That's it!"

CHAPTER 8
SPIN CONTROL

The sun was setting, and the kids didn't have much time until it was totally dark.

"What's the big idea, Arnold?" Keesha asked.

"We have another way to make the wheel spin," Arnold said. "In fact, we have two ways: water power and wind power."

"That's right, Arnold," Jyoti said. "When the force of the water in the waterfall pushed against it, the wheel turned on its own in the water."

"And when the wind caught it, the wheel spun on its own in the air, too," Keesha added.

"So to turn the rotor, we don't need to create pollution or pedal all night," Ralphie said.

"We need to find a way to use the power from the water and the wind," said Arnold.

"Yeah!" shouted the kids.

"Okay, you guys," Arnold said. "Let's do this!"

The kids found a windy spot near the riverbank. Keesha propped a wheel on a three-legged stand.

"We need something to catch the wind and make the wheel turn," Jyoti said as she held up a deck of cards. "These baseball cards should do the trick."

Jyoti carefully stuck cards between the wheel's spokes.

When all the cards were in place, Ralphie announced the next step: "Now we attach the wheel."

"And boom!" Carlos shouted. "The rotor spins through the wire coil, and then all the wheel-turning energy becomes electricity."

The wind caught the cards on the wheel. The cards flapped as they made the wheel spin faster and faster.

"Woo-hoo!" Arnold cheered.

He pulled out a long extension cord and attached one end to the generator. He carried the other end back to camp.

Meanwhile, more powerful stuff was happening at the waterfall. Wanda and Dorothy Ann were setting up another wheel near the rushing waters with cups attached to the spokes.

"The water will fill the cups and the weight of the water will turn the wheel," Dorothy Ann explained.

"What are we waiting for?" Tim said. "Let's go electric!"

The running water splashed into the cups. Everyone cheered as the power of the water made the wheel spin.

"It's working! Nice!" Wanda said.

She gave Dorothy Ann a thumbs-up. It was time for the next step.

Dorothy Ann pulled out another extension cord. She attached one end to the generator and carried the other end back to camp.

When Dorothy Ann reached the campsite, she found Arnold looking nervous.

"Are you okay, Arnold?" Dorothy Ann asked. "You seem scared."

"This is it, D.A.," Arnold said with a sigh. "If we fail, prepare to become monster chow!"

Arnold and Dorothy Ann attached the extension cords to the lights for the test run. The rest of the class returned just when Arnold was about to flip the switch. But first he had a few words.

"I just want to say that what we did today as a team was—so cool."

"Dude, it's dark," Ralphie interrupted. "Flip the switch!"

Arnold took a deep breath, then he and Dorothy Ann flipped the  switch. But as he looked around the campsite, his stomach flipped, too.

The kids waited but nothing happened.

CHAPTER 9
HAPPY CAMPERS

Arnold felt his heart sink inside his chest. Without lights, the Official Arnold Perlstein Monster Scaring Perimeter was an epic fail!

Just then—FLASH—the lights throughout the campsite turned on.

"Arnold, you did it!" Dorothy Ann cheered.

"We all did it," Arnold said. "Bright lights, clean power, and no Blot Monster!"

"Wahoo!" The class cheered.

The lights were up and there was no monster in sight. Now the class was ready for fun.

The Magic School Bus had turned into a giant camper.

"Pretty cool, right?" Ms. Frizzle asked. "It's eco-friendly and pollution-free."

"It's also monster-free," Arnold said. "That's the coolest part of all!"

"Ms. Frizzle, come roast marshmallows with us!" Keesha called.

The class sat around a big, roaring campfire. Ms. Frizzle walked over.

"I'd love to join you," she said. "I'll use my clean energy–powered magical mallow toaster!"

Everyone laughed as Ms. Frizzle caught flying marshmallows when Wanda gasped. "Uh-oh. What is that?" she asked.

She pointed to a dark, giant shadow looming over the camper.

"Oh no!" Arnold cried. "The Blot Monster came anyway!"

"But there's no pollution," Wanda said.
"And we have light," Carlos added.
"Everybody hide!" Arnold shouted.
The class went running in all directions.

"No need to scamper from the camper," Ms. Frizzle said. "That's our very own Liz Monster!"

Liz Monster?

Their class pet was just a tiny lizard, but she cast a huge shadow!

"See, Arnold?" Wanda said. "Everything is fine."

"For now," groaned Arnold.

The campfire crackled as the kids went back to some serious marshmallow roasting. Their class camping trip was a success, thanks to Ms. Frizzle, the Magic School Bus—and a few bright ideas!

GLOSSARY

Compass: an instrument that helps determine directions like north, south, east, and west

Electricity: a form of energy that helps power machines and devices

Enlightening: educational and informative

Exhaust: gases or steam produced by an engine

Inflated: filled up with air

Perimeter: the boundary of an area

Pollution: harmful materials that damage the environment

Power plant: a place where electricity is generated

Projector: a machine that shows slides or movies on a screen

Tentacles: long, flexible body parts that animals such as octopuses and squid have

Transform: to change into something else

Ask Professor Frizzle

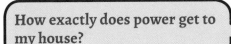 How exactly does power get to my house?

 It starts out in a power plant, which is a giant version of the generator Arnold made. Then the electricity generated there is carried along power lines to your house.

This book showed us wind and water power, but isn't the sun a clean energy source, too?

 You bet! In fact, solar panels can convert energy directly into electrical current. You don't even need a generator.

Are there other ways to make clean electricity?

 Yesarooni! Engineers are studying ways to harness power from the tides in the ocean and even from heat inside the earth.

What happens when we use up all the energy in the world?

 Well, we can't! Scientists say "Energy can neither be created nor destroyed." Instead it changes form into things like heat, light, and sometimes pollution. But even if it doesn't pollute, making electricity still costs money and resources, and we should always save as much as we can.

Why is renewable energy called "clean energy?"

 Great question! When people say energy is "clean," they mean it does not produce pollution like the gas generator in the story. Pee-yew!

Thanks for all your help, Professor Frizzle!

 These were some powerful questions. Now I have got to electric boogie-woogie on out of here!

The Magic School Bus
Rides Again

QUESTIONS and ACTIVITIES

1. The monster from Arnold's scary movie had fourteen eyeballs and giant tentacles! Draw your own creepy monster.

2. Why does Arnold go on the camping trip even though he is scared?

3. List some objects in your house that use electricity.

4. Why didn't the class want to use gasoline to power the generator?

5. How did Arnold feel when his class helped him power the lights?